Poems and Prayers

For the Very Young

A Random House PICTUREBACK®

Poems and Prayers

FOR THE VERY YOUNG

Selected and Illustrated by MARTHA ALEXANDER

Random House New York

Acknowledgments

The publishers have made every effort to locate the owners of all copyrighted material and to obtain permission to reprint the poems in this book. Any errors are unintentional, and corrections will be made in future editions if necessary. The publishers acknowledge with thanks permission received from the following to include the poems in this collection:

William Collins Sons & Co., Ltd. for four lines from "Thank You For The World So Sweet" by Edith Rutter Leatham. Doubleday & Company, Inc. and The Society of Authors as the literary representative of the Estate of Rose Fyleman for "Singing-Time" from *The Fairy Green* by Rose Fyleman. Copyright 1923 by Doubleday & Company, Inc. E. P. Dutton & Co., Inc. for "Stars" from *Stories To Begin On* by Rhoda W. Bacmeister. Copyright 1940 by E. P. Dutton & Co., Inc., renewal © 1968 by Rhoda W. Bacmeister. Vida Lindo Guiterman for "Sleepy Song" from *The Light Guitar* by Arthur Guiterman. Copyright 1923 by Harper & Row, Publishers, Inc., renewed 1951 by Vida Lindo Guiterman. Houghton Mifflin Company for "The Sun" from *All About Me* by John Drinkwater. Robert C. Jackson and Rand McNally & Co. for "The Sea Gull" by Leroy F. Jackson from *Child Life Magazine*. Copyright 1925, 1953 by Rand McNally & Company. The National Society for the Prevention of Blindness for "A Great Gray Elephant." G. P. Putnam's Sons for "Brooms" from *Everything and Anything* by Dorothy Aldis. Copyright 1925, 1926, 1927, renewed 1953, 1954, © 1955, by Dorothy Aldis. The Viking Press, Inc. for "Firefly" from *Under the Tree* by Elizabeth Madox Roberts. Copyright 1922 by B. W. Huebsch, Inc., renewal 1950 by Ivor S. Roberts. Western Publishing Company, Inc. for "Slumber Song" by Karl Simrock, adapted by Louis Untermeyer, from *The Golden Book of Poetry*. Copyright © 1959 by Western Publishing Company, Inc.; and for "God Made The Sun" by Leah Gale, "God Watches Us" by Gabriel Setoun, and "A Child's Prayer" by M. Betham Edwards from *Prayers for Children*—A Little Golden Book. Copyright 1942, 1952; by Western Publishing Company, Inc.

48 49 50

Singing-Time

I wake in the morning early
And always, the very first thing,
I poke out my head and I sit up in bed
And I sing and I sing and I sing.

—*Rose Fyleman*

Dear Father, Hear And Bless

Dear Father,
    hear and bless
Thy beasts
    and singing birds:
And guard
    with tenderness
Small things
    that have no words.

—*Unknown*

Clouds

White sheep, white sheep,
On a blue hill,
When the wind stops
You all stand still;
When the wind blows
You walk away slow,
White sheep, white sheep,
Where do you go?

—*Christina G. Rossetti*

A Child's Prayer

God, make my life a little light,
   Within the world to glow;
A little flame that burneth bright,
   Wherever I may go.

God, make my life a little flower,
   That giveth joy to all,
Content to bloom in native bower,
   Although the place be small.

God, make my life a little song,
   That comforteth the sad,
That helpeth others to be strong,
   And makes the singer glad.

—*M. Betham-Edwards*

Father, We Thank Thee

For flowers that bloom about our feet,
   Father, we thank Thee,
For tender grass so fresh and sweet,
   Father, we thank Thee,
For the song of bird and hum of bee,
For all things fair we hear or see,
Father in heaven, we thank Thee.

For blue of stream and blue of sky,
  Father, we thank Thee,
For pleasant shade of branches high,
  Father, we thank Thee,
For fragrant air and cooling breeze,
For beauty of the blooming trees,
Father in heaven, we thank Thee.

For this new morning with its light,
  Father, we thank Thee,
For rest and shelter of the night,
  Father, we thank Thee,
For health and food, for love and friends,
For everything Thy goodness sends,
Father in heaven, we thank Thee.

—*Ralph Waldo Emerson*

Song

The lark's on the wing;
The snail's on the thorn:
God's in His Heaven—
All's right with the world!

—Robert Browning

Peace Be To This House

Peace be to this house
And to all who dwell in it.
Peace be to them that enter
And to them that depart.

—Unknown

God Be In My Head

God be in my head
And in my understanding.
God be in mine eyes
And in my lookings.
God be in my mouth
And in my speaking.
God be in my heart
And in my thinking.

—Unknown

All For Thee

All for Thee,
  Dear God,
Everything I do,
  Or think,
  Or say,
The whole day long.
Help me to be good.

—*Unknown*

Table Blessing

God, we thank you for this food,
For rest and home and all things good;
For wind and rain and sun above,
But most of all for those we love.

—*Maryleona Frost*

Out In The Fields With God

The little cares that fretted me,
   I lost them yesterday,
Among the fields above the sea,
   Among the winds at play,
Among the lowing of the herds,
   The rustling of the trees,
Among the singing of the birds,
   The humming of the bees.

The foolish fears of what might pass,
   I cast them all away,
Among the clover-scented grass,
   Among the new-mown hay,
Among the hushing of the corn
   Where drowsy poppies nod,
Where ill thoughts die and good are born—
   Out in the fields with God.

—*Louise Imogen Guiney*

The Creation

All things bright and beautiful,
   All creatures, great and small,
All things wise and wonderful,
   The Lord God made them all.

Each little flower that opens,
   Each little bird that sings,
He made their glowing colors,
   He made their tiny wings.

The tall trees in the greenwood,
   The meadows where we play,
The rushes by the water
   We gather every day—

He gave us eyes to see them,
   And lips that we might tell
How great is God Almighty,
   Who has made all things well!

—Cecil Frances Alexander

Thank You For Summer

Thank you, God, for summer
   With all its flowers gay,
And birds that sing, and green grass,
   And butterflies that play
At hide and seek with clover,
   And blossoms on the trees,
And sunshine bright, and showers,
   And every cooling breeze.

Yes, thank you, God, for summer;
   And always at my play
Help me, Thy child, remember
   These gifts of Thine, I pray.

—Unknown

The Sun

I told the sun that I was glad,
  I'm sure I don't know why;
Somehow the pleasant way he had
  Of shining in the sky,
Just put a notion in my head
  That wouldn't it be fun
If, walking on the hill, I said
  "I'm happy" to the sun.

—*John Drinkwater*

A Kite

I often sit and wish that I
Could be a kite up in the sky,
And ride upon the breeze and go
Whichever way I chanced to blow.

—*Unknown*

Grace

Thank you for the world
    so sweet,
Thank you for the food
    we eat,
Thank you for the birds
    that sing,
Thank you, God,
    for everything!

—Edith Rutter Leatham

Who Has Seen The Wind?

Who has seen the wind?
   Neither I nor you:
But when the leaves hang trembling,
   The wind is passing through.

Who has seen the wind?
   Neither you nor I:
But when the trees bow down their heads,
   The wind is passing by.

—*Christina G. Rossetti*

Rain

The rain is raining all around,
It falls on field and tree,
It rains on the umbrellas here,
And on the ships at sea.

—*Robert Louis Stevenson*

Brooms

On stormy days
When the wind is high,
Tall trees are brooms
Sweeping the sky.

They swish their branches
in buckets of rain,
And swash and sweep it
Blue again.

—*Dorothy Aldis*

I'm Glad

I'm glad the sky is painted blue,
   And the earth is painted green,
With such a lot of nice fresh air
   All sandwiched in between.

                —Unknown

A Child's Prayer

Make me, dear Lord, polite and kind
   To everyone, I pray.
And may I ask you how you find
   Yourself, dear Lord, today?

          —John Banister Tabb

God Made The Sun

God made the sun
   And God made the tree,
God made the mountains
   And God made me.

I thank you, O God,
   For the sun and the tree,
For making the mountains
   And for making me.

—Leah Gale

The Sea Gull

I watched the pretty white sea gull
Come riding into town;
The waves came up when he came up,
Went down when he went down.

—Leroy F. Jackson

He Prayeth Best

He prayeth best,
    Who loveth best
All things both great and small;
For the dear God
    Who loveth us,
He made and loveth all.

—Samuel Taylor Coleridge

The Lord's Prayer

Our Father which art in heaven,
Hallowed be Thy name.
Thy kingdom come;
Thy will be done
On earth as it is in heaven.
Give us this day our daily bread,
And forgive us our debts,
As we forgive our debtors.
And lead us not into temptation,
But deliver us from evil:
For Thine is the kingdom,
And the power, and the glory,
For ever. Amen.

Firefly

A little light is going by,
Is going up to see the sky,
A little light with wings.

I never could have thought of it,
To have a little bug all lit
And made to go on wings.

—*Elizabeth Madox Roberts*

A Great Gray Elephant

A great gray elephant,
    A little yellow bee,
A tiny purple violet,
    A tall green tree,
A red and white sailboat
    On a blue sea—
All these things
    You gave to me,
When you made
    My eyes to see—
        Thank you, God.

—Reprinted by permission of
The National Society for the
Prevention of Blindness, Inc.

Stars

Bright stars, light stars,
Shining-in-the-night stars,
Little twinkly, winkly stars,
Deep in the sky.

Yellow stars, red stars,
Shine-when-I'm-in-bed stars,
Oh how many blinky stars,
Far, far away!

—*Rhoda W. Bacmeister*

Twinkle, Twinkle, Little Star

Twinkle, twinkle, little star,
How I wonder what you are!
Up above the world so high,
Like a diamond in the sky!

When the blazing sun is gone,
When he nothing shines upon,
Then you show your little light,
Twinkle, twinkle, all the night.

—*Jane Taylor*

God Watches Us

God watches o'er us all the day,
At home, at school, and at our play;
And when the sun has left the skies,
He watches with a million eyes.

—*Gabriel Setoun*

I See The Moon

I see the moon,
And the moon sees me.
God bless the moon,
And God bless me.

—*Unknown*

Night

The sun descending in the west,
The evening star does shine,
The birds are silent in their nest,
And I must seek for mine.

—*William Blake*

Good Night Prayer

Father, unto Thee I pray,
Thou hast guarded me all day;
Safe I am while in Thy sight,
Safely let me sleep tonight.

Bless my friends, the whole world bless;
Help me to learn helpfulness;
Keep me ever in Thy sight;
So to all I say good night.

—*Henry Johnstone*

Sleepy Song

Every little nail
   Asleep in the wall,
Every little lamb
   Asleep in the stall,
Every little flower
   Asleep in the dew,
Oh, my little darling,
   Go to sleep, too!
Oh, my little darling,
   Go to sleep, too!

—*Arthur Guiterman*

Bedtime Prayer

Now I lay me down to sleep,
I pray Thee, Lord, Thy child to keep:
Thy love guard me through the night
And wake me with the morning light.

—*Unknown*

Lullabye

Sleep, baby, sleep,
Thy father guards the sheep;
Thy mother shakes the dreamland tree,
Down falls a little dream for thee:
　Sleep, baby, sleep.

Sleep, baby, sleep,
The large stars are the sheep;
The little stars are lambs, I guess;
The gentle moon's the shepherdess:
　Sleep, baby, sleep.

—Unknown

Slumber Song

Go to sleep and good night;
In a rosy twilight,
With the moon overhead
Snuggle deep in your bed.
God will watch, never fear,
While Heaven draws near.

—From the German by
Karl Simrock
Adapted by Louis Untermeyer

The Gift

What can I give Him,
   Poor as I am?
If I were a shepherd,
   I would bring Him a lamb.
If I were a wise man,
   I would do my part.
But what can I give Him?
   Give Him my heart.

—Christina G. Rossetti

Good Night! Good Night!

Good night! Good night!
Far flies the light;
But still God's love
Shall flame above,
Making all bright.
Good night! Good night!

—*Victor Hugo*